To Ron and Claire,
for giving me the confidence
to do what I love.

 little bee books

A division of Bonnier Publishing
853 Broadway, New York, New York 10003
Copyright © 2016 by Stacey Previn
All rights reserved, including the right of reproduction in whole or in part in any form.
LITTLE BEE BOOKS is a trademark of Bonnier Publishing Group, and associated colophon
is a trademark of Bonnier Publishing Group.
Manufactured in China   LEO 0616
First Edition   10 9 8 7 6 5 4 3 2 1
Library of Congress Cataloging-in-Publication Data
Names: Previn, Stacey, author. Title: If Snowflakes Tasted Like Fruitcake / by Stacey Previn.
Description: New York : Little Bee Books, [2016]
Identifiers: LCCN 2015049671 | ISBN 9781499801804 (hardback)
Subjects: | BISAC: JUVENILE FICTION / Cooking & Food. | JUVENILE FICTION /
Imagination & Play. | JUVENILE FICTION / Concepts / Seasons.
Classification: LCC PZ8.3.P9155 If 2016 | DDC [E]—dc23
LC record available at https://lccn.loc.gov/2015049671
ISBN 978-1-4998-0180-4

littlebeebooks.com
bonnierpublishing.com

IF SNOWFLAKES TASTED LIKE FRUITCAKE

Stacey Previn

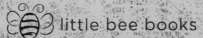

little bee books

If snowflakes
tasted like

sugar plums....

they'd be dancing in my head.

If snowflakes
tasted like

oatmeal . . .

they would
get me out of bed.

If snowflakes tasted like

honey...

then we wouldn't
need the bees.

If snowflakes
tasted like

plump figs....

I would shake
them off the trees.

If snowflakes
tasted like

cocoa...

they would warm me
to my toes.

If snowflakes
tasted like

whipped cream...

they would tickle me on my nose.

If snowflakes
tasted like

chestnuts . . .

I would roast them
by the fire.

If snowflakes
tasted like

gingerbread . . .

I would make a cookie choir.

If snowflakes
tasted like

popcorn...

I would string them all together.

If snowflakes
tasted like

marshmallows...

they'd be lighter than a feather.

If snowflakes
tasted like

apples . . .

I would bake them in a pie.

If snowflakes
tasted like

peppermint....

I'd wish more fell
from the sky.

If snowflakes
tasted like

gumdrops...

the roof is
where I'd stay.

If snowflakes
tasted like

fruitcake...

we would give them all away.

If snowflakes
tasted like

noodle soup....

I would slurp them just for fun.

But snowflakes
taste like

winter . . .

So I'll catch them
on my tongue!